A RAY OF LOVE

NANCY HARRISON

ILLUSTRATED BY
JOHN JOSEPH

KIDS

BROWN BOOKS KIDS

A Ray of Love

Brown Books Kids
Dallas, TX / New York, NY
www.BrownBooksKids.com
(972) 381-0009

A New Era in Publishing®

Publisher's Cataloging-In-Publication Data

Names: Harrison, Nancy, 1975- author. | Joseph, John, 1985- illustrator.
Title: A ray of love / Nancy Harrison ; illustrated by John Joseph.
Description: Dallas, TX ; New York, NY : Brown Books Kids, [2020] | Interest age level: 004-
007. | Summary: "After graduating from star school, Sunny is thrilled to find out he will
be the star for Earth-the biggest job a star can have! But when he sees how some of the
people of Earth treat each other, he is discouraged, and he has to figure out what can be
done to fight the violence and hatred he sees. Join Sunny in discovering what powerful
force can rid the world of this negativity for good"--Provided by publisher.
Identifiers: ISBN 9781612544496
Subjects: LCSH: Sun--Juvenile fiction. | Earth (Planet)--Juvenile fiction. | Violence--Prevention-
-Juvenile fiction. | Love--Juvenile fiction. | CYAC: Sun--Fiction. | Earth (Planet)--Fiction. |
Violence--Fiction. | Love--Fiction.
Classification: LCC PZ7.1.H37 Ra 2020 | DDC [E]--dc23

ISBN 978-1-61254-449-6
LCCN 2020903387

Printed in Malaysia
10 9 8 7 6 5 4 3 2 1

For more information or to contact the author, please go to
www.MarkoBooks.com.

DEDICATION

To my husband, Jason.
Your encouragement in all areas of my life
has let me accomplish so much.

ACKNOWLEDGMENTS

I want to thank my husband for his constant encouragement and excitement on each step of this journey.

Thanks to my parents, Djuro and Marta Markovic—because of the constant determination and discipline they bestowed upon us growing up, fulfilling goals in my life has been second nature.

A thank-you to the team at Brown Books for taking a chance on me and all the people behind the scenes that played a huge part in getting my book perfected and published.

Another big thanks to my illustrator, John, who has captured Sunny in the perfect "light."

Sunny was a special star.
He had a BIG HEART, and
he always wanted to know
what he was shining for.

Sunny trained with all the other little stars in a special school deep in space, where if stars do well, they are given jobs shining on worlds. Sunny learned to shine as bright as he could.

"A sun's job is to give WARMTH and LIGHT," Sunny's father told him.

Sunny grew, and his heart grew too. There was WARMTH and LIGHT in his heart, and it helped him shine a little brighter every day.

When the last day of training came, the teachers stood in front of the students at the star school, ready to assign them their jobs across the universe.

Sunny stood taller than all the other students. "You have worked so hard and grown so big," the principal told him. "You shine so bright that you will have the biggest job a star can have. You will be the sun for Earth."

All Sunny's friends and classmates cheered.
But the loudest cheer came from his father.

When the day came for Sunny to start his new job in the skies of Earth, his father walked him part of the way. "You are going to make a great sun, son," he said. He hugged Sunny goodbye.

Sunny rose above the skies of Earth to start SHINING.

Sunny was proud and happy to
be the sun for Earth. He watched
couples holding hands. He saw
children running, playing, and
laughing together. He saw
dogs chasing toys. Their
owners smiled when
the dogs brought
back the prize.

But then Sunny saw angry people. He saw people hurting one another with their words. Some of them hurt one another with weapons. He watched little children crying because they were so sad.

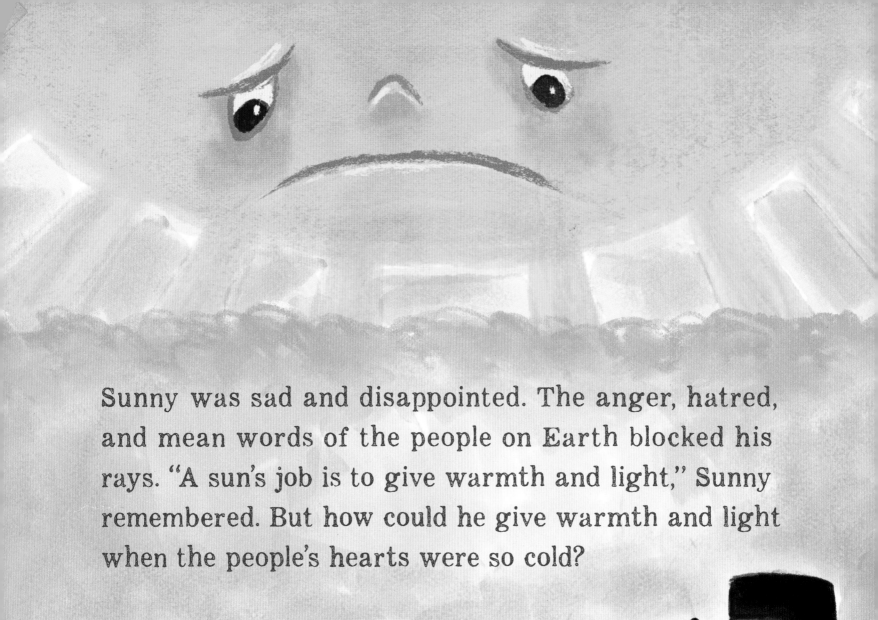

Sunny was sad and disappointed. The anger, hatred, and mean words of the people on Earth blocked his rays. "A sun's job is to give warmth and light," Sunny remembered. But how could he give warmth and light when the people's hearts were so cold?

When Sunny went to bed that night, he closed his eyes tight and hoped. He wished and prayed, "Let me rise tomorrow to see a BETTER DAY."

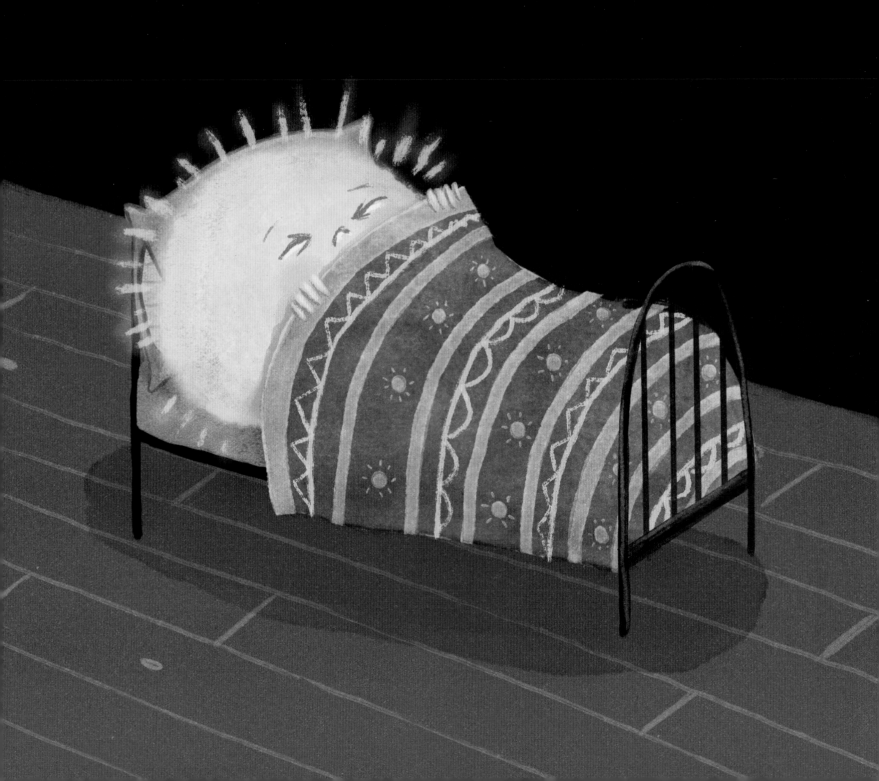

The next day, when Sunny rose, the Earth was covered in clouds. Fog, snow, and rain blocked his rays. "I'm not strong enough to shine through this!" he said.

But he tried.

After a long day, he headed home. He was defeated.
He lay in bed, and he hoped. He wished and prayed,
"Let me rise tomorrow to see a BETTER DAY."

The next day, Sunny saw more clouds. There was more fog and snow and rain. "Anger, hatred, and mean words block my rays," Sunny said. "Now even the weather keeps me from shining."

At the day's end, Sunny had been defeated again. He didn't want to hope. He could not wish or pray. But then something changed inside his heart. "I shouldn't have to SEE a better day," he decided. "I need to BE a better day."

The next morning, Sunny was excited to go to
work. He rose high in the sky. He saw the clouds
and the fog, the snow and the rain. But this time,
Sunny decided not to be defeated.

He took a deep breath. He remembered everything he had learned in star school, and he shone with all his strength.

Brighter and brighter Sunny shone. The clouds and fog, snow and rain began to melt away.

But then he realized he had only changed the weather. Anger, hatred, and mean words still blocked his rays.

He could give warmth and light to the Earth. But Sunny still did not know how to shine warmth and light into the hearts of its people.

Sunny sighed. Then he looked again, and he saw families eating together. Friends were laughing together. Some children smiled as they played and listened to the stories of their parents. Sunny's heart warmed and grew.

"That's it!" Sunny yelled. "LOVE can fix the anger, hatred, and mean words. It's LOVE that shines warmth and light on the heart!"

So that night, before Sunny closed his eyes to sleep, he hoped. He wished and prayed, "Let me rise tomorrow to SHINE LOVE on the new day."

The next day, when Sunny saw the arguing people, the people fighting and hating, he looked harder. He focused his rays on one small, sad child sitting alone in the park.

She stretched out and smiled in his warmth.
She grew happier and ran off to the jungle
gym to play with other children.

The love Sunny had shared spread on the playground and followed every child there home that night.

Sunny was happy as he went to lay his head down. He had found how he could help.

"All it takes is one person," he realized.
"One person's love to make the hearts
of the people warmer and lighter."

And before he went to sleep, he hoped.
He wished and prayed, "Let me rise and
SHINE LOVE on someone new each day."

ABOUT THE AUTHOR

Born and raised in Windsor, Ontario, Nancy Harrison moved to the United States in 1997. In 2006, Nancy a registered nurse, and her husband, Jason, general surgeon, established a surgical practice Highlander Surgical Associates, and they have owned and operated the practice together ever since.

Writing has always been one of Nancy' passions, and after years of encouragement from her husband, she decided to publish *A Ra of Love*, her first children's book. It is Nancy' ambition to bring more innocence and love to the world through her stories.

Nancy and her husband live in Mansfield, Texas.

ABOUT THE ILLUSTRATOR

John Joseph is a *New York Times* best-selling illustrator of many book for children. He lives in Colorado, where the sun shines over three hundre days per year. When not making art for books, you can find him teaching art to children and playing with his two little boys.